Up up You Go Jo!
Copyright © 2021 by Mariam Shapera

All rights reserved. No part of this publication may be reproduced, distributed, or transmitted in any form or by any means, including photocopying, recording, or other electronic or mechanical methods, without the prior written permission of the author, except in the case of brief quotations embodied in critical reviews and certain other non-commercial uses permitted by copyright law.

Tellwell Talent
www.tellwell.ca

ISBN
978-0-2288-5073-1 (Hardcover)
978-0-2288-5074-8 (Paperback)

Dedication

For my children Joseph, Marla, and Matthew.
To my husband for supporting me.

Late one evening, after he had finished composing his freestyle music, Jo felt proud. His music consisted mainly of half notes, quarter notes, and eighth notes.

"Time to get ready for bed," his mother called.

After a strong windy night, Jo hopped out of bed, excited to play on his piano.

He stared at his music sheet. *What happened to my music?* he thought.

His music sheet was still on the stand but without the notes!

He searched all over the house, but no notes could be found.

"I'm sure you remember your music. You can just write it again," said his mother.

His father thought of something that might cheer Jo up. He suggested they go to the local fair which was visiting town that weekend.

At the fair, Jo refused to go on any of the rides.

There were many balloons of different colors and shapes. Jo had an idea!

"Mom! Dad! Can I please buy 10 balloons?" he asked eagerly.
"10 balloons?" asked his mother. "Whatever for?"

Could my musical notes have flown out through the window and traveled up into space? Jo thought.

"Last night, I think my music may have flown out of my room and up into space! I can use those 10 balloons to fly up to space and bring them back," Jo replied hastily. His parents agreed to the plan.

That windy evening, standing outside his house, Jo carried two parachutes on his back and wore a small saddle bag to place his notes in. After his father handed him the 10 balloons, Jo was swept up higher and higher into the evening sky. He felt excited but also determined to find every single missing music note.

Up he went, higher and higher, into complete darkness...

As he held on tightly to the balloons, he heard a strange sound behind him and turned his body around. In front of him was a small, gray alien spaceship with a one-eyed green creature sitting in the middle of it. Jo thought it was strange that this creature should look so different from him.

"Hello," said Jo. "Sorry to bother you, but have you seen any musical notes flying around here?"

The strange-looking creature remained silent. Then the glass cover over the center of his small spaceship opened and a half musical note came out of it! Jo could not believe his eyes! He grabbed the note and put it in his saddle bag. He looked up to thank the alien but saw that he had already disappeared into dark space.

Amazing! thought Jo.

Just then, he heard a rumbling sound growing louder and louder. Straight ahead of him he could see a dark rock-like object flying closer and closer to him. Balanced on the asteroid, he saw another one of his lost notes! It was an eighth note. Jo's eyes popped wide open with excitement. He leaned over and grabbed it just as the asteroid flew past him and then vanished away.

"Whoosh, whoosh" were the next sounds he heard. Turning, he saw three or maybe four very bright objects of blue, green, and yellow colors. They looked as if they were dancing around each other.

"Shooting stars!" Jo shouted to himself. He headed in their direction. As he got closer, he saw a few more of his notes: one on each of the stars. They were all quarter notes. He could also feel the heat from the shooting stars soaring towards him. He grabbed his notes quickly, being careful not to burn his hand. *Beautiful!* he thought.

Jo knew all his planets very well, but famous Saturn was the most beautiful of them all! *Wow! Those rings look like 100 rainbows around the gas planet,* he thought. Still holding his balloons, Jo flew closer to the rainbow rings.

He could see they were actually made of rainbow-colored rocks and there he saw two of his notes. These were quarter and eighth notes. He grabbed those also.

By now, Jo was feeling tired. He was about to drift off to sleep while still holding his balloons when he heard a loud thundering vroooom.

Jo opened his eyes wide and looked around. He could no longer see Saturn but a white rocket! The rocket soared closer and closer and a small door on its side opened. Jo could see an astronaut in a white suit smiling and waving at him.

The astronaut's large arm stretched out and grabbed Jo's hand and pulled him inside the small rocket. Once inside, Jo let go of his balloons. He watched them drift out of the rocket and become smaller, eventually turning into many dots in space.

The rocket door closed behind Jo. He looked around and saw buttons and computers on all the walls. The astronaut smiled, opened a large drawer, pulled out a quarter note and two eighth notes, and then handed them to Jo.

"Jo, darling, are you awake?" Jo's mother asked.
Jo, lying in his bed, slowly opened his eyes.
"Where am I, Mom?" asked Jo.
"You are home of course, dear," replied his mother.
Jo looked around at the familiar sight of his room.
He got out of bed and slowly stood on his feet.
"Breakfast is ready!" said his mother.

As she left the room, Jo turned around and looked at his piano. There, on the music sheet, were all his notes in their perfect position as he had composed them.
He could not believe his eyes!
He could not believe how much joy he felt!
He closed his eyes for a few seconds and then opened them again to make sure that the notes were still there, and they were. *Was it all just a dream?*

Jo was about to leave his room when a strap-like object from behind his piano caught his eye. It was his bag's strap. He pulled his bag out and remembered that in his dream, if it was a dream, he had used this bag to collect his musical notes. Inside the bag was empty except for a rainbow-colored rock about the size of a marble! Just like the ones he saw on Saturn's rings!

CPSIA information can be obtained
at www.ICGtesting.com
Printed in the USA
LVHW071536100721
692368LV00007B/247